Emma Lou

the Yorkie Poo

BREATHING IN
THE CALM

KIM LARKINS

Loving Healing Press
Ann Arbor, MI

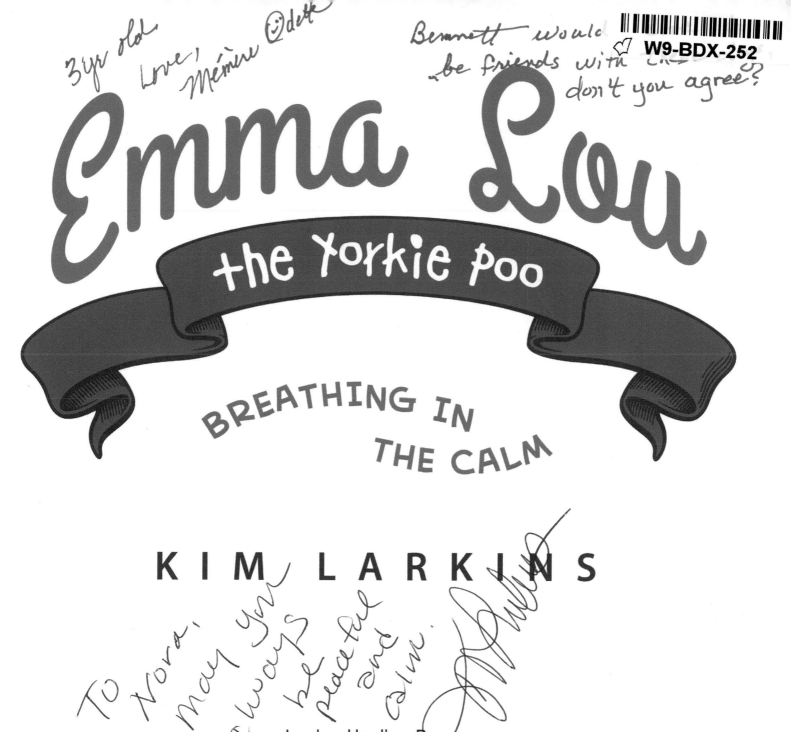

Library of Congress Cataloging-in-Publication Data

Names: Larkins, Kim, author.
Title: Emma Lou the Yorkie Poo : breathing in the calm / by Kim Larkins.
Description: Ann Arbor, MI : Loving Healing Press, [2019] | Summary: Emma Lou
   the Yorkie Poo worries most of the time until she and her absentminded
   friend, Pearl, learn focused breathing from Gigi the Gentle Ginormous
   Giraffe.
Identifiers: LCCN 2019013207 (print) | LCCN 2019016652 (ebook) | ISBN
   9781615994588 (Kindle, ePub, pdf) | ISBN 9781615994564 (pbk. : alk. paper)
   | ISBN 9781615994571 (hardcover : alk. paper) | ISBN 9781615994588 (eBook)
Subjects: | CYAC: Anxiety--Fiction. | Breathing exercises--Fiction. | Yorkie
   poo--Fiction. | Dogs--Fiction. | Animals--Fiction.
Classification: LCC PZ7.1.L3514 (ebook) | LCC PZ7.1.L3514 Emm 2019 (print) |
   DDC [E]--dc23
LC record available at https://lccn.loc.gov/2019013207

Published by
Loving Healing Press
5145 Pontiac Trail
Ann Arbor, MI 48105

Toll free: 888-761-6268 (USA/CAN)
Fax: 734-663-6861

www.LHPress.com
info@LHPress.com

Distributed by
Ingram (USA/CAN/AU), Betram's Books (UK/EU)

Dedication

To Guyer and Giavanna,

Keep breathing in the calm.

Emma Lou the Yorkie Poo was a very nervous dog that worried most of the time. The tiny black dog with big brown eyes had big worries to match. Emma Lou's friends were always trying to think of new ways to help her stop worrying but found it very frustrating at times.

They would say, "Don't worry, Emma Lou, that's not ever going to happen. You're just silly. Stop worrying, and go play with Pearl."

Emma's friends didn't understand that telling her not to worry was not helpful. It caused her to think about her worries more and become even more anxious.

Emma Lou's best friend, Pearl, was a very kind and quiet but quite active dog. She listened to Emma Lou's worries and felt sad for her. Pearl didn't understand why Emma Lou worried so much. She wanted to help her but didn't know how. Sometimes Pearl would get distracted. She would forget what Emma Lou was saying, and her mind would wander off to something else.

One day on the way to the dog park, Emma Lou and Pearl saw their friend Caleb, a very athletic calico cat, flying through the air. He landed in front of them and stopped them in their tracks.

"What are you two dogs doing?" questioned Caleb.

"What are we doing?" barked Emma Lou. "What are you doing almost flying in to us? You could have hurt us, or we could have tripped and skinned our knees. What if Pearl walked right in to you? She never looks where she's going!"

"Well, that sounds silly," replied Caleb. "Why would any of that ever happen? Emma Lou, you worry too much!"

"I know," said Emma Lou, sounding quite discouraged. "That's what everyone tells me, but I don't know what to do!"

Now Caleb is a bossy cat, so he told Emma Lou exactly what he thought. "I think you need to go see my friend, Gigi the Gentle Ginormous Giraffe. She was very helpful to me. I was not always this brave, and I didn't know how to fly until Gigi helped me and gave me this colorful calico cape."

"What do you think, P—" Emma said as she looked around. "Where did she go?" worried Emma Lou.

Emma spotted Pearl already at the dog park, twirling in circles with Beatrice Butterfly and her band of Merry Musical Monarchs.

"Pearl!" Emma Lou barked in her most frustrated voice. "Come over here!"

Pearl scampered back to Emma Lou and Caleb.

"Did you want something, Emma Lou?"

"Caleb thinks we should go visit her friend Gigi to help me with my worrying. What do you think?" Emma Lou was not quite sure. "What if she thinks I'm silly like everyone else?"

"I double dog dare you two to give it a try!" Caleb taunted.

Pearl jumped up and down with excitement, saying, "If Caleb thinks it will help, let's give it a try!" She was always willing to help her friends and wondered if Gigi could also help her when she gets distracted.

"Follow me!" ordered Caleb, and off they ran toward Gigi's house.

Emma Lou and Pearl scampered along as fast as they could to keep up with Caleb. He was very fast indeed! Through the park, across the bridge, and under the bushes they ran until they came upon a bright yellow house.

On the door, a sign read "Please Come In, and Kindly Remove Your Shoes."

"Shoes? How can we take off something we don't have?" worried Emma Lou.

"Emma Lou," sighed Pearl, "it's going to be okay. Dogs don't need shoes. Let's just go inside."

So, they quietly crept inside. They could see a circle of others sitting on a very soft blue rug.

"Come in, come in," said Gigi.

"She sure is ginormous," thought Emma Lou.

"Come and join my friends, Patrick [a chubby, pink pig] and your friend Caleb," said Gigi. "Caleb told us you would be joining us."

Emma Lou and Pearl found a spot on the rug and listened to Gigi. "Let your eyes close or focus on a spot on the rug, and we will begin to learn together how to feel calm and peaceful."

Gigi gently tapped her singing bowl with her tiny mallet and said, "Listen to the sound until you can no longer hear it. Begin to breathe in and out, and focus your mind where you feel your breath."

Gigi noticed that Pearl was glancing around the room. "If you lose your focus, notice that you are distracted, and come back to breathing in and out."

"Now, take a deep breath in through your nose until you feel it way down in your belly, and hold it as I count to four. One-two-three-four," Gigi whispered. "Now, slowly blow your breath out through your mouth, one-two-three-four. Continue to breathe in and out, and try your best to stay focused on your breath."

Gigi waited for a few minutes, occasionally reminding Pearl to keep breathing, and then said, "Gently open your eyes."

Emma Lou could not believe how relaxed she felt. She thought, "I almost forgot that I was worried about coming here. I hope I can come back and try this again."

Gigi thanked them all for visiting her and told them they were always welcome back. She reminded them, "You now know how to slow down your breathing, which will help relax your mind and body. You can practice anywhere that you breathe!"

Emma Lou and her friends quietly walked out into the warm summer breeze. Emma Lou felt very relaxed until she realized Pearl was missing!

"Pe—!" she started to yell, but stopped herself. She saw Pearl across the meadow jumping and spinning with Beatrice and the monarchs.

"It's okay," Emma thought. "She will come back when she's ready. I will wait under this tree, listen to the wind blowing through the leaves, close my eyes, and practice breathing in the calm."

About the Author

Kim Larkins is a Licensed Clinical Social Worker in private practice. For the past thirty years, Kim has dedicated her career working with children and families in the mental health and human services field. Most recently, Kim has worked in educational settings focused on the development of mindfulness skills in the classroom. Research shows that mindfulness in education improves attention, emotional regulation, compassion for self and others, and overall well-being for both students and teachers. *Emma Lou the Yorkie Poo: Breathing in the Calm* will introduce parents, therapists, educators and children to some of the many benefits of a mindfulness practice.

Kim has a Master of Social Work degree from the University of Maine. She is also licensed in Maine where she works and lives. Kim has two adult children, Sarah and Theron and two grandchildren, Guyer and Giavanna. She enjoys travel, music, quilting, and the serenity and pleasures found in nature. You can contact her by email at kimlarkinslcsw@gmail.com or on Facebook @kim.larkins.author.

CPSIA information can be obtained
at www.ICGtesting.com
Printed in the USA
BVHW091409180819
555935BV00004B/13/P